FREYA'S FANTASTIC SURPRISE

Libby Hathorn • Sharon Thompson

SCHOLASTIC
HARDCOVER

SCHOLASTIC INC.

New York

Text copyright © 1988 by Libby Hathorn.
Illustrations copyright © 1988 by Sharon Thompson.
All rights reserved. Published by Scholastic Inc.
SCHOLASTIC HARDCOVER is a registered trademark of Scholastic Inc.

No part of this publication may be reproduced in whole or in part, or stored
in a retrieval system, or transmitted in any form or by any means,
electronic, mechanical, photocopying, recording, or otherwise, without
written permission of the publisher. For information regarding permission,
write to Scholastic Inc., 730 Broadway, New York, NY 10003.
First published in 1987 by Ashton Scholastic Pty Limited (Inc. in NSW), P.O. Box 579,
Gosford 2250. Reprinted by arrangement with Ashton Scholastic Pty, Ltd., Australia.

Library of Congress Cataloging-in-Publication Data
Hathorn, Libby.
Freya's fantastic surprise / Libby Hathorn; illustrated by Sharon
Thompson.
p. cm.
Summary: Jealous of the big surprise her friend Miriam has told
everyone at school, Freya begins inventing one fantastic surprise
after another for their school's News Time, until her mother
supplies her with a real surprise to announce.
ISBN 0-590-42442-4
[1. Envy—Fiction. 2. Honesty—Fiction. 3. Schools—Fiction.
4. Friendship—Fiction. 5. Babies—Fiction.] I. Thompson, Sharon,
1958- ill. II. Title.
PZ7.H2844Fr 1989
[E]—dc19   88-28165
CIP
AC

ISBN 0-590-42442-4
12 11 10 9 8 7 6 5 4 3 2 1   9/8 0 1 2 3 4/9
Printed in the U.S.A.   36
First Scholastic printing, April 1989

On the way to school, Freya's friend, Miriam, told her she had a surprise to tell at News Time and it was fantastic!

Freya asked if the surprise was

    a Mars bar
    or a pop-up book
    or a treasure chest
    or a bike,

but Miriam said it wasn't any of these.

Then Freya asked Miriam was her surprise

    new shoes
    or a heart-shaped pad and pencil
    or having your ears pierced
    or a special medicine to make your warts go away?

"No," said Miriam, glancing at the wart on her thumb.
"It's better than any of those!"

Then she smiled that slow smile
that always made Freya so mad,
and she said,

"I'll say at News Time and not before."

When Mrs. Colvin asked if anyone would like to tell some news, Miriam almost jumped out of her chair.

She told the class that she had a *fantastic surprise.* Nobody would ever guess unless they had seen her mother in the sporting goods store last week buying something awfully big.

"An axe?" Jason Medway called out.

"No," said Miriam.

Miriam's eyes were shining as she took a deep breath and said all at once, "My mother bought me my own green-two-sleeper-tent-with-a-door-and-windows-and-even-a-tiny-front-verandah."

"Fantastic," Jason Medway called out, and the class clapped.

"It's not just pretend," Miriam added. "It's for adults and things."

The class clapped again.

Miriam sat down looking very pleased. She glanced sideways at Freya and smiled her slow smile.

On the way home from school, Freya checked with Miriam about the tent. Sometimes Miriam made things up. But the green-two-sleeper-tent-with-a-door-and-windows-and-even-a-tiny-front-verandah was true all right!

"But you can't go inside or anything," Miriam said. "Not yet! Only special people get to go inside and Jason Medway's first and then a whole lot of other kids. You can go on the list, though," Miriam said kindly.

"No thanks," said Freya, and she went home.

"I want to tell a surprise at News Time," Freya told her Dad as he read to her that night.

Dad looked over the top of his funny new half-glasses and said, "What about your tooth falling out last week?"

But Freya said, "Kids' teeth falling out isn't much of a surprise!"

"It's got to be a *fantastic* surprise," Freya told Dad as he tucked her into bed.

"Lie there and think about it for a while," Dad said.

The next day at News Time, Freya put her hand up.

"I have a surprise," she said, staring hard at Miriam.

"We'd love to hear your surprise, Freya," Mrs. Colvin said.

"I have a *guinea pig*," Freya said, and the class clapped.

Miriam's hand shot up. "What does it look like?" she asked.

Freya thought for a moment. "Well, it's white, and it has blue eyes…and it has six legs."

The class laughed.

"That's an unusual guinea pig," the teacher said.

On the way home from school, Miriam said, "You don't have a guinea pig at all! That's a lie, Freya. Everyone knows guinea pigs have four legs. You don't have a guinea pig at all!"

The next day at News Time Freya put up her hand again.

"I have a surprise," she said, staring hard at Miriam.

"We'd love to hear your surprise," Mrs. Colvin said.

"I have a horse!" Freya announced and the class clapped.

"Where do you keep your horse?" Miriam asked.

"In the garage at the bottom of our apartment house," Freya answered quickly.

"Isn't it a bit dark in there for a horse?" Jason asked.

"Oh no! There's a light in there you know."

On the way home from school Miriam said, "That's a lie, Freya. Everyone knows you don't have a horse! You wouldn't be allowed to keep a horse in the garage even with the light on."

It was on the last day of the week that Freya put up her hand again at News Time.

"I have…"

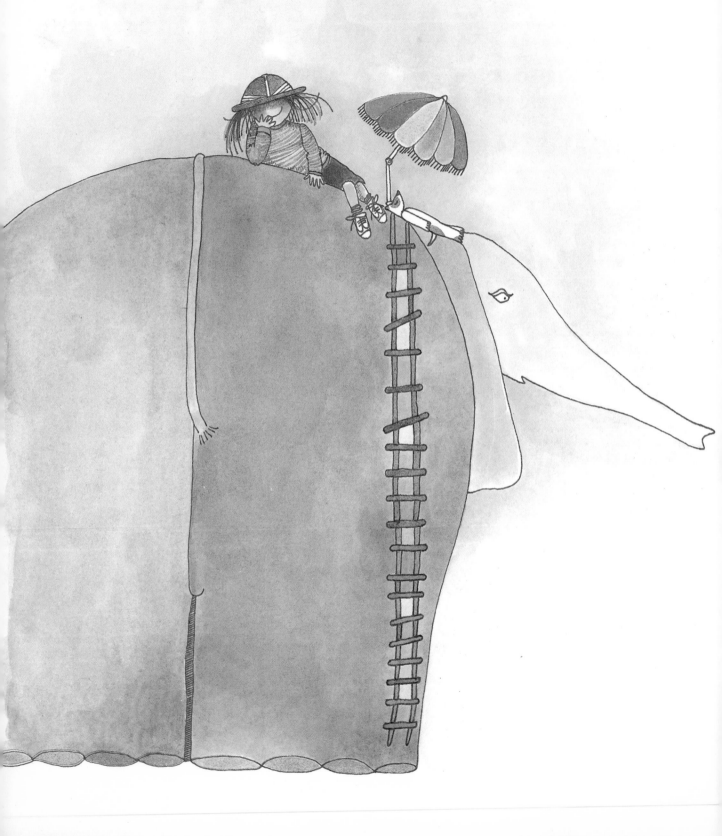

Everyone stared hard at Freya. She swallowed and thought hard for a moment.

Then she said, "I have an *elephant.*"

The class gasped.

"It's only a baby one, though," Freya added quickly.

Timothy and Kylie snickered, but Jason and Miriam laughed out loud.

"Are you sure you don't mean a picture of a baby elephant?" Mrs. Colvin asked.

Freya looked down at her sneakers.

"Yes," she whispered, "I have a picture of a baby elephant."

The class was very quiet.

On the way home from school Miriam said, "You'd better stop making up these surprises Freya, or you'll get in trouble. And I mean big trouble!"

That night Mom and Dad wondered why Freya kicked the plant with the tiny green tomatoes on it and punched the pillow and refused to eat the pizza Dad brought home.

Then she told them. "Everyone in the class knows I made them all up—the guinea pig and the horse in the garage and the baby elephant. Even Mrs. Colvin. And I'm never going back to school again!"

Then Mom leaned over and whispered something in Freya's ear…

"Wow," Freya said, and then, "Fantastic!"

She ate every bit of her pizza and asked for another slice. "How long till Monday?" Freya asked, "I can't wait to tell my *fantastic* surprise!"

On Monday, Freya squirmed so much Mrs. Colvin said she was like a can of worms or a box of monkeys. At News Time she waved her hand so excitedly that Mrs. Colvin asked her first.

The class sighed.

"I have a fantastic surprise," Freya said loudly and clearly, looking straight into Mrs. Colvin's eyes. "And no one could ever guess it, not unless they've been talking to my mom and dad."

"Can you taste it?" Toula called out.

"No," Freya said with a slow Miriam kind of smile.

"Well, can you see it?" Jason asked.

"Not yet," Freya answered mysteriously.

Then she took a deep breath. "My mom's going to have a baby. A real baby. And we're buying a cradle for the baby. And the baby gets to sleep in my room and share my toys."

"Fantastic," said Jason Medway, and the class clapped.

Miriam put up her hand. "Is it a boy or a girl?" she asked.

The class laughed.

"I guess that will be another fantastic surprise Freya will have for us," Mrs. Colvin said.

On the way home from school, Miriam asked, "Is it true about the baby?"

Freya looked solemn. "It's true! You can come home right now and ask my mom and dad."

Miriam was quiet for a moment. Then she said, "When the baby's born, well, after a while your mom and dad might get sick of it. You could bring it over to my place and we could look after it in the tent!"

"I'd have to ask," Freya said.

"Why don't you come and check out the tent right now?" Miriam said.

"I'd have to ask," Freya said, and then she ran all the way home.

She threw her bag down so hard it skidded across the kitchen floor.

"Everyone got a real surprise about the baby. I can't stay. I'm going to check out where we can put the baby in Miriam's new green-two-sleeper-tent-with-a-door-and-windows-and-even-a-tiny-front-verandah!"

"Fantastic," she heard Dad call after her as she dashed down the dark back stairs and out into the sunshine.